For George and Phyllis who love bears

A VANESSA HAMILTON BOOK
Copyright © 1990 Wendy Smith

First published 1990 by
PAN MACMILLAN CHILDREN'S BOOKS
A division of Pan Macmillan Limited
Cavaye Place, London SW10 9PG and Basingstoke
Associated companies throughout the world

Picturemac edition published 1992

A CIP catalogue record for this book is available from
the British Library

ISBN 0-333-54924-4

Printed in Hong Kong

SAY HELLO, TILLY!

Wendy Smith

SAY HELLO, TILLY!

Wendy Smith

M
MACMILLAN CHILDREN'S BOOKS

Tilly was getting ready for a party. She didn't really want to go.

"I don't like parties," she moaned.

"I hope you're not going to be a party-pooper," warned Mother.

It was Benny's birthday party. He was not a brainy bear, but he had a kind heart, and lived only a little way down the road.

Sometimes he was Tilly's dancing partner at Madame Nijinska's Saturday class.

Tilly loved dancing, but not with Benny. His paws always smelled of chicken soup in the *pas de deux*.

And he was useless at lifts.

But the real reason for not wanting to go to the party was that Tilly felt shy. Apart from Benny, there would be no one she knew. None of her friends from school was going. Benny had invited them all but they didn't really like him.

"Sorry, Benny, but I think I'm getting measles," lied Lisa.

"I've too much homework," fibbed Noeleen.

"'Fraid I can't, Benny. I'm busy that day," said Gloria quite truthfully.

"Do I really have to go?" whined Tilly. "I won't know what to say to anyone."

"You mustn't be so backward in coming forward," Mother advised her. "Just say hello and smile. Now, hurry, or we'll be late."

Benny's father opened the door.
"Say hello to Mr Waters and Benny, Tilly," said Mother.
Tilly said nothing.

"Benny'll think you don't like him," Mother whispered.
"'Lo," mumbled Tilly.
"And?" prompted Mother.
Tilly blushed deeply.
"Girls!" muttered Benny, running off to play.
"Happy birthday," said Tilly – too late.

Tilly had a lovely present for Benny. But she was too shy to give it to him.

"I'll take that, my dear," said Benny's father. "Come in and join the fun!"

Everyone was crowded round Benny's new computer game.
"Excuse me," Tilly whispered politely.
But no one even heard her.

So Tilly sat like a wallflower on the edge of the room,
wishing she was at home.

Just then the doorbell rang. There was a puff of green smoke and in burst Mrs Magic, the conjurer.

"Now, I need someone to be my assistant," said Mrs Magic. "Who's it going to be?"

"Me!" cried Benny.

"Behave!" snapped Benny's mother.

"Me! Let me!" cried Flora, Dora, Johnny and Carlos.

"No," said Mrs Magic firmly. "How about that little bear in the corner?"

"Who, me?" said Tilly.
Everyone stared at her, mad with envy.
"No," she said bashfully. "I don't want to."

So it wasn't Tilly who was sawn in half.
A stout bear with glasses called Nora was.

But when it came to pulling rabbits out of a hat,
Nora was hopeless.

I should have said yes, thought Tilly glumly.

For her last act, Mrs Magic produced, in a shower of stars, a splendid birthday tea.

There was a frantic scramble for the food. By the time Tilly reached the table, just one jelly was left. It had clean run out of wobble.

Tilly was wondering whether to start at the head or tail when Mrs Waters interrupted her thoughts.

"Tilly, dear, this is Pablo. He has just arrived from Spain and has no one to talk to."

The room suddenly seemed very quiet.

Tilly stared at Pablo. Pablo stared at Tilly. Each waited for the other to say hello.

He looks shy, she thought. It must be lonely for him being in a different country.

"Hello," she said, plucking up her courage.

Pablo smiled at her. "I no like parties," he said.
"I don't either," agreed Tilly.

"But dancing is fun," she added, hearing the sounds of Mr Waters' Gypsy Band in the garden.

"*Si*. I like it too," said Pablo, smiling broadly.

So Tilly and Pablo took to the patio.

Pablo proved himself to be a wild and wonderful dancer.

Tilly enjoyed herself so much that she forgot all about being shy.

(Pablo's paws, she noticed, smelled of distant orange groves.)

"Hurray!" cheered everybody when the music finally stopped.

"Bravo!" cried Father who had come to take Tilly home.

"This is my best friend, Pablo," said Tilly.

"And that was a lovely party, Benny," she added, waving goodbye.

Tilly and Pablo became the best of friends. On Saturdays they went to Madame Nijinska's class where they were star turns at the flamenco – an exciting gypsy dance.

And afterwards, Tilly helped Pablo practise a little English while he taught her some useful words in Spanish.

"Saying hello . . ." said Tilly,
". . . with a smile," added Pablo,
". . . is a sure way of making friends," finished Tilly.
"Hola! Hello!"

Also available by Wendy Smith in Macmillan

GINGER THE WHINGER

Other Picturemacs you will enjoy

For a complete list of Picturemac titles write to

Pan Macmillan Children's Books
18–21 Cavaye Place, London SW10 9PG